# MOGO'S FLUTE

WEEKLY READER CHILDREN'S BOOK CLUB

*presents*

# MOGO'S FLUTE

*Hilda van Stockum*

*Drawings by Robin Jacques*

THE VIKING PRESS  NEW YORK

Fic 1. Africa—Kenya

Copyright © 1966 by Hilda van Stockum

All rights reserved

First published in 1966 by The Viking Press, Inc.
625 Madison Avenue, New York, N.Y. 10022

Published simultaneously in Canada by
The Macmillan Company of Canada Limited

Library of Congress catalog card number: 66–11911

Weekly Reader Book Club Edition

*To the teachers and pupils of
Kianda College, Nairobi.*

# CONTENTS

7

# THE THAHU

Mogo was a little Kikuyu boy who lived in Kenya, East Africa. He lived in a village of round thatched huts surrounded by vegetable patches, or *shambas*.

Where he lived there is neither summer nor winter. There are only long rains and short rains, with dry harvest periods in between. The sun rises every morning at seven, and at seven in the evening it goes down again, all the year round.

Mogo still slept in his mother's hut, with his sister Njoki and the baby Mtoto. Most other boys of his age were already considered old enough to sleep in their father's hut. That's where Karanja and Kimani, Mogo's elder brothers, slept. But Mogo had delicate health. When he was an infant foolish women had praised him too much. That had attracted evil spirits, or perhaps it had angered a jealous ancestor. A spell, or *thahu*, had fallen on him. He had sickened, and seemed to be dying. Mogo's

9

father had hurried to the Mundo-Mugo, the wise man. The wise man had given him a powerful charm, and Mogo had lived. But the charm was not able to banish the thahu altogether, so Mogo didn't grow tall and strong like his brothers. He cried often, though his mother never left him but carried him with her on her back when she worked. It was only by singing that she could quiet him. He loved sounds and soon learned to imitate the calls of the rainbird and the francolin.

His mother nursed him through many fevers and would not let him out of her sight. As long as she sang he was happy, so she sang to him all day long. She sang of the great god Ngai, who reigns alone in the skies, and of the beautiful world he made with his hands. She sang of the first man Gikuyu, who came out of a hole in the ground when Ngai called him, and of his wife Moombi. They lived happily together in a place surrounded by wild fig trees. Nine daughters were born to them, but as there were no other people in the land, where were they to find husbands for their nine daughters? Gikuyu and Moombi lifted their hands to Mount Kere-Nyaga, where Ngai dwelt, and they told him their trouble. And Ngai answered that if they made a sacrifice under the largest fig tree, he would take care of their daughters.

As soon as the smoke of the sacrifice had blown away, nine beautiful young men stood under the sacred tree. Then the father and mother and the nine daughters and the nine young men feasted for many days, and the daughters married the young men. Those were the beginnings of the nine tribes of the Kikuyu people. All this Mogo learned through his mother's songs, without even knowing it, when he was still quite small.

When he grew a little older his mother would play games with him.

"Are you ready?" she would ask. Then Mogo would say, "Yes, I am ready."

"Here's a riddle, then. I have two goatskins, one dark, one light. I stretch them out to dry, and look . . . they come together."

At first Mogo did not know the answer to this riddle, but after a while he learned to say, "The earth and the sky."

Another riddle was, "Who is always falling down but never dies?" and the answer was "The moon."

Mogo learned many riddles this way. He also learned to answer the questions his father asked him.

"What is your name?" his father would say. At first he answered, "Mogo," but his father taught him to answer, "Mogo, son of Maina, grandson of Karanja."

"Who is your grandfather?"

"He is an elder. He has many goats, many shambas, and many huts. When he was young he was a great warrior and killed many Masai. His grandchildren are scattered like the blossoms of the jacaranda tree."

It was like another game. Through his father's questions Mogo learned the history of his tribe, the wars and the valiant deeds of his ancestors.

Sometimes Mogo asked questions himself.

"Father, if you went on digging and digging, where would you end up?"

"In the country of the spirits," his father told him.

"Do the spirits ever get angry?"

"Yes, and then they make the earth tremble."

Mogo's brother Karanja was good at playing the flute, or *motoriro* as it is called in Kikuyu. Mogo spent many hours listening to him. He asked Karanja to play so often that at last Karanja made him a little flute of his own and taught him how to blow a tune on it.

"He learns quickly, this one," Karanja told his mother. "For all he is skinny like a locust."

At first, his parents were pleased when Mogo played the flute because it kept him quiet and happy. But after a while, when he would do nothing except sit on his favorite rock and make music, they began to worry. It was wrong for a boy not to join his *riika*—the group of boys his own age. It was true that he was not good at the games, but at least they would give him exercise. Now his limbs were getting weak from sitting on that rock.

He was not strong enough for the long walk to school and back. That meant that he would never learn the foreigners' magic of talking with marks on paper. Unlike Karanja and Kimani, he would never work in the city and bring back shillings.

It's all because of that flute, thought his mother, and one day she hid it. But when Mogo could not find his flute he fretted himself into a fever and she had to give it back to him. The family decided there was nothing to be done about it. Mogo still had his thahu.

Mogo knew about his thahu; he knew he was not like other children. No one expected him to hoe or weed, and he was not allowed to fetch water or herd goats. He was only "poor Mogo," and people would have to look after him until he died.

Mogo's father was a strong man. He had killed lions and leopards. Their skins hung in his hut along with his shield and spears. Sometimes Mogo sneaked inside his father's hut and timidly fingered the weapons. It would have been good to be like his father and brothers, to do manly deeds, and to sleep here beside them and be spoken to with respect. But that would never happen, because of his thahu.

Karanja and Kimani were like their father. On holidays they went hunting with him or helped him clear a part of the forest. They were tall, with smooth brown skins and white teeth. When they played with little Mtoto, they would look at him with pride, but they would say, "What an ugly, weak little fellow he is." Mogo knew they did that to avoid the evil that had fallen on himself for being praised too much.

Once, when Mogo was in bed, he heard his parents discuss him.

"What's to become of him?" his father asked. "It would have been better if he had died at birth. He is fit for nothing but playing the flute. How will he live?"

"He plays the flute well," murmured his mother.

"What good is that to him?" grumbled his father. "The tune he blows goes into the air and vanishes—it neither sprouts bananas nor breeds goats. He is worse than a girl-child, who at least brings a bride price when she marries."

Mogo listened the way he listened to the rain rustling on the grass roof, or the goats snuffling in a corner of the hut. He felt about his thahu the way he felt about night coming after day or seedtime after harvest. If it had not been for his sister Njoki, he would never have shaken the tree of destiny and forced it to drop good fruit on him. He might still be sitting in his mother's hut, answering riddles.

One day during the millet harvest, when the whole village was busy haying and cutting grain, Mogo sat on his favorite rock and played the flute. Many birds had come to listen to him. They had lit on his head and shoulders or were hopping about his feet. Birds and small animals did not fear him, for he never made rough movements. Mogo felt happy, as always when playing. The thahu seemed to leave him then. He was filled with life, good life, the same life that made the birds hop and sing, that blew the white banners of clouds across the sky and set the millet rippling.

That life Mogo breathed into his flute, and the flute lifted it in a golden thread of sound which climbed up to the snows of Mount Kere-Nyaga, where, perhaps, the god Ngai wound it up to keep with his treasures.

There was a scrabbling noise as Njoki clambered up the rock. She was carrying Mtoto on her back and bending with his weight. She addressed Mogo politely, as befitted a younger sister.

"Son of our mother who was born before me," she said, "everyone else is working, but you are only pleasing yourself."

Mogo took the flute from his mouth. The thread of sound snapped and some of the birds flew away.

"Daughter of our mother who was born after me," he said, "what great work are *you* doing, then?"

"I'm minding the baby," she said.

14

"Well, I'm minding the birds," Mogo answered and began to play again.

Njoki stamped her foot on the rock. Her foot was bare and made no noise, but it showed she was angry.

"No one wants you to mind birds. You should be chasing them away with stones so they won't eat the millet," she shouted. "Even tiny boys can do that. Why do you not try to be helpful? Why do you let everyone call you 'poor Mogo'? Why do you let the neighbors whisper that you are a burden to your parents? Why? Why? Why?" And she kept stamping her silent foot.

Mogo lowered his flute.

"What else can I do?" he asked, feeling sorry for himself. "You know there is a thahu on me from an evil spirit."

"I don't believe it," shouted Njoki. "I am sorry for you whenever you are really ill, but you are not ill now, just lazy. You like being petted and having your own way. I'm sure there is nothing wrong with you, nothing!"

To Mogo's surprise, Njoki began to cry. Mogo scrambled to his feet and patted Njoki's shaking shoulders.

"There, there," he said. "Do not be sad. I don't mind. It's Ngai who made me, and he must not be troubled with our grief."

"First you say it's the fault of an evil spirit, and now you say it's the good Ngai. You don't make sense." Njoki sobbed, rubbing her eyes with the tip of her shawl. The baby woke and began to whimper. Njoki bent and straightened her knees in a jogging motion which rocked him to sleep again.

"If you think there is a thahu on you," she said more gently, "why don't you go to the Mundo-Mugo and have it taken off?"

"Didn't father try that already?" asked Mogo.

"Perhaps this is a thahu you can only loosen yourself," said Njoki. "Why don't you go to him right away and see what he says?"

"To the Mundo-Mugo? Alone?" There was a quaver in Mogo's voice. The Mundo-Mugo was terribly old and lived by himself in the forest. No one knew his thoughts or could predict what he would do. There were those who said that he spirited away little children.

"Why not?" asked Njoki. "Are you afraid?"

"No, no," said Mogo hastily. "But I have nothing to offer him. Father brings him a gourd of honey beer or a bag of beans. All I have is my flute and I'll *never* part with that."

"You may have my necklace," said Njoki.

Mogo was silent, remembering the beautiful scarlet beads, the gift of an aunt, which were Njoki's only treasure.

"You can't do that," he protested.

"Yes I can," said Njoki. "Come to our hut and I'll give it to you. I want you to find out for sure. I don't think you are 'poor Mogo' at all. I think . . . I think you could be 'wonderful Mogo.' " She turned her face away.

"I'll go," promised Mogo, his heart beating faster. "But why do you care so much?"

"Because you are my brother," said Njoki.

# THE
# MUNDO-MUGO

Mogo did not tell his mother where he was going. She might find some reason to stop him. Most women kept their children away from the Mundo-Mugo, fearing his magic.

So Mogo sneaked away quietly, wondering at his own courage. He had never been close to the Mundo-Mugo, though he had seen him at ceremonies from afar: a man like a goat, bony and bearded, with compelling eyes. Mogo knew that to find him he only had to follow the path that led to his hut, a path worn by the feet of many people in trouble.

First Mogo passed the hut of old Wangari, who had no husband any more, nor teeth, nor hair. She sat patiently in her doorway every day, waiting for death. Mogo feared her, for she said things that came from nowhere and went nowhere.

"Boy, boy," she croaked as Mogo passed. "Where are my dreams? Did you take them? Come and play for me, bring them back to me, I want sleep."

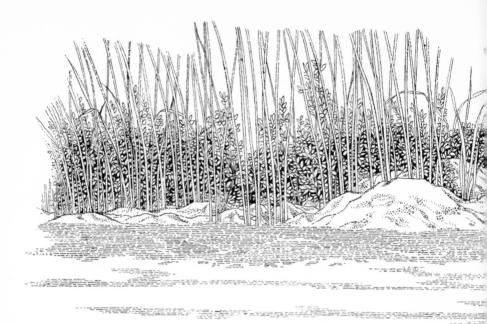

"I'll come later," Mogo promised. It was better not to annoy her, for old people have powerful magic. How else could they have fooled the evil spirits for so long?

Some children were playing on the road. They called to him when they saw him.

"Poor Mogo, poor Mogo, play us a tune!"

Mogo ran. If he lingered they would ask questions, and he did not want anyone to know where he was going.

He already saw the river gleaming between bamboo bushes. It widened there into a little lake. Blue waterlilies grew along its edges. Mogo looked for the old hippopotamus who lived there, but he was a lazy beast and you did not often catch sight

of him. Mogo wanted to see him, as it would give him luck on his journey. The hippopotamus was the emblem of Mogo's tribe. It was forbidden to hurt the animal or eat its flesh, and whomever the hippopotamus looked upon was favored by fortune.

Mogo wondered if the hippopotamus would come to him, like other animals, when he played. He took the flute out of his woolly hair, where he kept it when not in use, and put it to his mouth.

The flute on which he had learned had been made of bark, with only four holes. But bark flutes don't last long, and later Karanja had made him this lovely flute out of bamboo, with many holes.

19

Mogo took care to blow gently and evenly. Like tiny soap bubbles, the first soft tones floated over the water. They became fuller and rounder as Mogo went on playing. Flamingoes walking on pink stilts among the blue lilies snaked their necks to listen. Several giraffe peeked over bushes and around trees. A fat rhinoceros waddled out of the underbrush on the other side of the lake, bringing her baby son. A curious marabou bird stalked up behind Mogo and stood motionless on one leg. But though Mogo was flattered with so much attention, none of these creatures would bring him luck.

Mogo's fingers flickered and his music pattered like rain, but there was no sign of the old hippopotamus. Mogo shook his head and blew silver arrows of sound which finally pierced the small ears of the hippopotamus. The still reflections in the water rippled to pieces and the monster heaved itself out of the mud, lifting its huge head. Its bulging eyes winked at Mogo and its shiny skin shivered. Then with a snort the hippopotamus swam away as if to say "It is too noisy here for me."

But Mogo was satisfied. He had done everything he could to make his journey a success. There was a fluttery feeling in his stomach, as if he had swallowed a live frog. He shook his flute dry and stuck it back into the close thatch of his hair, which held other treasures—a stick of sugarcane and a stump of charcoal.

Mogo walked along the river as far as he could. The river was a cheerful companion. It was itself silent, having no rocks to talk to, but it was loud with the murmur of the birds that nestled at its borders. Presently, however, he had to leave it and follow the path into the dark forest.

It was cold under the thick shelter of leaves. Mogo's bare feet padded on the path. Mogo heard the stirring of many creatures and felt hidden eyes watching him. He remembered what his grandmother had told him. Long, long ago there had been dwarfs in the forest. They had fought the Kikuyu people, but whenever the Kikuyu had tried to pursue them, the ground had suddenly swallowed the dwarfs up. They had a magic word and could open the ground at will. Then, one day they disappeared and were seen no more. Mogo's grandmother said that Ngai had punished them for fighting the Kikuyu people. He had made the dwarfs forget the magic word that opened the ground so they had to remain locked up down there forever.

Mogo wondered if one day they might remember the word and come back.

The farther Mogo went into the forest, the more uncomfortable he felt. It was not a good place to walk alone. Perhaps he should not have gone without telling his mother. What if something happened to him? The frog in his stomach seemed to be dancing wildly. Why did he listen to a younger sister? Why was he doing this?

What if the Mundo-Mugo got angry with him? He could see deep into a person's heart; you could hide nothing from him. He knew what was to come and what had gone before. For him, time was not a rushing river but a still pool that reflected the face of Ngai.

Mogo remembered how the Mundo-Mugo had brought rain when the dry season had lasted beyond planting time. The rain had come down in torrents on the people who were going home from the ceremony.

Once, when a thahu had fallen on the village and many people had become ill, the Mundo-Mugo had sewn the sickness into the belly of a goat and buried it.

Another time, Mogo's father had found the droppings of a hyena right in front of his hut, a sign of very bad luck. But the Mundo-Mugo had given him a powerful charm and nothing bad had happened after all.

So the Mundo-Mugo must be a good man and not evil, as some people said.

Still, it was an awesome thing to be going to him alone. Mogo shook his head over his own foolishness at obeying a sister, younger even than himself.

He wondered if he shouldn't turn back . . . but it was a long way to have gone for nothing, and what would Njoki say? She would call him a coward.

Mogo went on with dragging feet, pushed by the thought of Njoki's scorn and pulled a little by curiosity. He could at least have a peep at the Mundo-Mugo before he ran back.

But when he saw the Mundo-Mugo sitting in front of his small hut, he did not think of running. The Mundo-Mugo sat motionless. He did not turn his head when Mogo approached. It was as if he had captured stillness and held it, so that it spread around him the way warmth spreads around a fire. Mogo felt trapped in it. He could neither move nor speak. He began to breathe slowly and deeply. The frog in his stomach stopped jumping.

For a long time Mogo stood there, held by the silence until the Mundo-Mugo stirred and blinked, and looked around.

"Ah," he said, and under his heavy lids his eyes held a luminous amber light as they looked at Mogo.

22

Mogo bowed and bent his head. "Peace be to him who speaks with Ngai," he said.

"Peace be to Mogo, son of Maina, grandson of Karanja," the Mundo-Mugo answered. "What is your trouble?"

"It is only this," said Mogo. "I have a thahu. I am often ill and I am not strong. I can only play the flute. But my younger sister says I am just lazy, that I am not 'poor Mogo,' that I could be 'wonderful Mogo.' She sends you these beads if you will tell me how."

Mogo took the beads from around his neck. The Mundo-Mugo stretched out a gnarled hand and took them. For a moment he warmed himself on their glow, and then he slid them inside his garments.

"So you can play," he said. "Play for me."

Mogo was always ready to do that. He took the flute out of his hair, and sitting cross-legged on the ground, he played a song of hope. He played the dark thread of his thahu and the bright thread of the wise man's powers, twining and untwining them until the dark thread snapped and the song ended in a little fountain of light.

Meanwhile the Mundo-Mugo had taken some beans out of his magic basket and was throwing them into patterns on a dried animal skin. When Mogo had finished he nodded.

"You were right to come," he said. "I have a message for you." He sat silent for a moment, fingering his beard.

"Why are shadows darker as light grows brighter?" he murmured. "Why is a curse also a blessing, and a gift a loss? Praise Ngai, peace be with us.

24

"Your thahu is your destiny. It is both your hardship and your joy. Without it, you would not play the flute as you do. Would you give up your flute in exchange for better health?"

"No, oh, no," cried Mogo, clasping the flute to his narrow chest.

The Mundo-Mugo nodded, smiling a little. Then he suddenly looked stern.

"A tree cannot grow straight when the wind is always blowing from the same direction. Your ancestors are angry with you."

Mogo sucked in his breath. His mother had warned him ever since he was a baby not to provoke his ancestors. They were powerful. Though their bodies had been eaten by hyenas, their spirits had joined the spirits of the wind. You could not see them, but they were everywhere, watching you.

"W-w-what have I done?" he stammered.

"It's what you have *not* done," the Mundo-Mugo said sternly. "Even with a thahu, you are still a member of your tribe. You must take your part in the work and games of your tribe. Otherwise you bring no honor to your ancestors."

"But I am no good at those things," said Mogo. "The only thing I do well is play the flute."

"It is not enough," said the Mundo-Mugo. "You must learn to do the other things too. A lone bee perishes and one twig cannot make of itself a basket."

"B-but my thahu?" whispered Mogo.

"Everyone has a thahu. That is life. You must learn to master it."

"But how can I do that?" asked Mogo, bewildered.

25

"Don't ask me," said the Mundo-Mugo, shifting the magic beans. "A chicken must peck itself out of its own egg. But remember, your ancestors are watching you. If you keep on neglecting your duties to play the flute, it will be taken away from you. Now I have a riddle for you.

"What is good to have, better to lose, and best to find again?"

Mogo stood frowning.

"I don't know," he said. "What is the answer?"

"You must discover it for yourself," said the Mundo-Mugo. "When you have it, come back and tell me. Now I must rest, I am tired, so run along."

The Mundo-Mugo closed his eyes. When they no longer lit up his face it looked as dark and still as a wooden mask.

Mogo tiptoed off and pondered all the way home the strange sayings of the wise man.

# MOGO TRIES

"What did he mean, I must master my thahu?" asked Mogo. He and Njoki were talking about Mogo's visit to the Mundo-Mugo. Their morning shadows stretched thin over the red clay of the yard. All around them their father's goats capered, waiting for Kunia, the herdsboy, to take them to pasture.

"I don't know," said Njoki. "But I've heard people say that the Mundo-Mugo was very ill as a child and that he cured himself by his own magic."

"I have only my flute," said Mogo, scratching a billy goat between its horns. "And he says I must not always play it."

"No," said Njoki. "You must help Father so that people can't whisper that he has a useless son." Mogo nodded.

"You must also help Mother," Njoki went on, "and not tease her for food all the time, the way Mtoto does."

"That is true," said Mogo, letting the goat nibble at his fingers.

"And you should help us when we work in a group. You sat
on your rock and played while we were building Kuria's hut."

"I remember," said Mogo, fondling the goat's ears.

"And when we had our festival of games, you didn't even try
to run races with the other boys. You just made music."

"It is true," said Mogo. "But if you tell me any more I'll
hit you."

So Njoki did not tell him any more.

Kunia came to fetch the goats. Mogo embraced the billy goat.
"Go off, Thaai," he said. "Eat your stomach full."

Thaai was his favorite among his father's goats. He was called

28

Thaai, which means *peace,* in the hope that it would tame him. He was a fierce billy goat, but he loved Mogo, who had once found him entangled in a thornbush and had patiently picked him out of it. He let Mogo ride on his back, and now and again, when he was in an angry mood, butting his horns and kicking up dust, Mogo was able to quiet him with his flute. Mogo felt envious of Kunia. He would have loved to be a herdsboy, out all day with his goats and his music. But his father didn't think him strong enough.

Wistfully Mogo watched the goats trot off after Kunia. He fingered his flute. He wanted very much to send up sounds like glad birds into the blue of the sky, but he was afraid. The Mundo-Mugo had said that if he played instead of doing his duty, his ancestors would take away his flute. He did not want that to happen. He looked uneasily about him, which was foolish, for his ancestors were invisible unless they took the shape of some animal.

The safest thing was to obey them, but what *was* his duty? He walked across the warm, dry land to his father, who was busy making a new shamba for Mother to grow more vegetables in.

"Baba," he said, "can I help you?"

His father stopped working and leaned on his digging stick. "Poor Mogo," he said. "Your arms are too weak. But I thank you for your offer. Go to your mother. Perhaps there is something you can do for her. And watch where you are going. I saw a big snake just now. It got away before I could kill it."

Mogo's father looked very powerful as he stood there, his bare arms and legs bulging with muscles. Mogo felt ashamed that he had offered to help. He walked slowly to his mother's hut.

"Maita, is there something I can do for you?" he asked.

"Oh, Mogo, yes, there *is*. You must know that Wambui, your cousin, has just had her baby, and I have promised to help her this morning. I should have kept Njoki in, but I forgot. She has gone off to weed the shamba. Please fetch her for me so that I can leave her in charge of the house."

"Can't I look after the house?" asked Mogo.

His mother laughed. "Poor Mogo, a fine mess you'd make of it!"

"Why? It's not such hard work," said Mogo. "I've seen you do it. You just sweep a bit and stir the pot and mind the baby. I can do that."

Mother laughed again. "It sounds easy, the way you say it," she admitted, stirring the porridge of corn and beans as she spoke. "But why do you suddenly want to do woman's work?" She licked the spoon. The *posho* smelled good, but Mogo did not ask to lick the spoon too. He knew that when a boy licks a spoon it makes a coward of him.

"I went to the Mundo-Mugo yesterday," he said. "Because of my thahu. And he says that my ancestors want me to help more. They don't want me to be always playing the flute."

His mother looked at him with awe. "You went to the Mundo-Mugo, all by yourself?"

"Njoki thought it would be a good idea," Mogo said.

"Well!" His mother regarded him thoughtfully. "Maybe it is true, what the Mundo-Mugo said. Maybe we've been treating you too much like a baby. All right, I will trust you. But it is a solemn trust, you understand? I do not leave just anyone to guard my hut."

"No, I see that," said Mogo, looking grave.

"Very well, then. The first thing to remember is that the fire must not go out. It's the sacred fire of our home, and letting it go out by accident brings bad luck."

Mogo nodded. "I know that," he said.

"The other thing is that babies have to be watched. They are very quick. Don't take your eyes off Mtoto."

"I won't," said Mogo.

"The third thing is our dinner. It must not cook too long. After a while you must take the pot off the hearthstones and put it aside. But don't on any account stir it."

"Why not?" asked Mogo curiously.

"Because then you will never get a wife," said his mother.

Mogo resolved to remember that. He wanted a wife when he grew up, to cook for him and fetch water and carry burdens and weave cloth and make clay pots and weed the shamba and do all the other useful things that women did.

"How long must I leave the pot on the fire?" he asked.

His mother smiled. "I'll show you," she said. She dug a big hole with her digging stick outside the hut. Then she took the water gourd which Njoki had filled that morning at the river, and poured water into the hole.

"It will take a while for the water to sink into the ground," she said. "When all the water is out of the hole, it will be time to take the pot from the fire."

Wrapping her shawl round her head, Mother left the house.

Mogo felt like a juggler who has been told to keep three balls in the air at once. Mtoto might have been a beetle the way he scuttled about on all fours. Mogo had to pull him away from his mother's grass-cutting knife, from the gourd with honey beer, and from the fire. When the water in the hole his mother had dug had all sunk into the ground, leaving it pitted like a honeycomb, Mogo lifted the heavy pot from the fire and put it on the ground.

Then, looking around, he saw that Mtoto had got into the precious salt pot and eaten a fistful of salt. Mogo scolded him and wiped his face, but soon after, the baby got sick all over him, and Mogo had to clean up the mess as well as he could, using the rest of the water from the water gourd. By that time it was necessary to put more sticks on the fire. Now I see why Mother laughed when I said she had an easy job, he thought.

Mogo felt an itch to play the flute, and that might also amuse the baby. But he was never allowed to play indoors, as that is sure to bring evil spirits upon a household. So he took the baby outside. But the minute he sat down to play, the baby crawled off.

Mogo saw the hole his mother had dug and got an idea. He made the hole a little larger and put Mtoto in it. Then he filled it up. Now Mtoto was buried up to his armpits and could not move. At first he cried, but Mogo gave him a banana to eat. Then Mogo sat down and played tunes for the baby, the tunes he had loved when he was young. Soon he got so absorbed that he forgot everything else.

## Mogo Tries

The fire in the hut burned greedily at first, biting away at the sticks, chewing out the middles until the scarred ends dropped into the glowing ashes. A few blue flames, looking for food, wandered about fitfully and finally went out.

Mogo went on playing.

Mtoto had put his thumb in his mouth and was sucking it. His eyelashes went up and down sleepily, like butterflies' wings. Mogo went on playing.

A black mamba snake which lay coiled on a high branch of the eucalyptus tree felt the vibrations of the music and began to move. It swayed to the rhythm of Mogo's playing, gently uncoiling itself. Then it slithered down the tree.

Mtoto had fallen asleep, his head resting on his fat little arms. The snake began to pour itself on the ground, flowing like a dark stream straight toward Mtoto.

And then, luckily, Mogo saw it. It was now quite close to the baby. Mogo could find nothing nearby with which to kill the snake. And he had no time to dig Mtoto up and carry him off. There was only one thing to do . . . distract the snake's attention and try to charm it away from the hut.

He got up and made motions to make sure the snake saw him. The snake stopped pouring and stiffened, its neck like a pole in the air, its tongue flickering like black lightning.

It was turning away from Mtoto.

Mogo began to play loudly and monotonously, the sing-song music he had heard an Indian snake charmer use once when he had been to the market with his mother. He had practiced it for days afterward and remembered it well.

The snake began to dance to its rhythm and then it started pouring again, away from the baby this time and in Mogo's direction.

Little drops of sweat pricked on Mogo's nose, but he went on playing as he slowly retreated from Mtoto and the hut and backed into the bushes that edged the shamba. His heart felt like a captive bird, knocking to get out. He played on, retreating foot by foot. He felt cool leaves brush past his naked legs, and here and there thorns caught at his skin or the cloth of his shorts, but he did not care where he was going as long as the mamba snake followed him and kept away from Mtoto.

Even when Mogo had got the snake deep enough into the woods for Mtoto to be safe, what could he do but go on playing? If he stopped, the mamba would strike him, surely, and there was such poison in his bite that even the Mundo-Mugo would not be able to cure him.

So Mogo played and played and played till his trembling fingers slipped on the flute.

Perhaps it is not a snake at all, but my angry ancestor, he thought. Perhaps he is making me play against my wish, to punish me. He wondered, in that case, if his ancestor would go so far as to bite him, but you couldn't be sure. The best thing was to go on playing. So Mogo played and played, with great fear in his heart.

When the shadow of the eucalyptus tree hit the roof of the hut, Mogo's mother arrived. She found Mtoto half buried and asleep. She dug him out, made sure he was all right, and hushed his cries. She found the hut unwatched, the fire out, the salt spilled, and the water gourd empty. A great anger raged inside her. She took her digging stick and ran to find Mogo. It was not difficult to tell where he was. Flute sounds were coming out of the woods at the back of the hut.

"Mogo, you son of bad luck," she shouted. "You breeder of trouble and disturber of spirits, where are you? Wait till I lay my stick on your idle bones. I'll make posho of them!"

She shouted so furiously and made such noise crashing through the bushes that the snake could not fail to hear her. It was suddenly gone, like a drop of rain in the ground. All the angry mother saw was Mogo, playing the flute.

# MOGO
# RUNS AWAY

When you are sore from being beaten with a digging stick and still sorer from feeling that it was done unjustly, you do not always see things straight.

To Mogo it seemed as if the weight of the sky had fallen on him. Never before had his mother been so angry with him. It had been impossible to tell her what had happened. It was like talking into a big wind; his words were blown away.

Oh, yes, he understood the misfortune of letting the fire go out; he also knew that ants might have eaten Mtoto, the way Mogo had left him half buried. But if his mother had listened when he tried to tell her about the snake, would she then have said she was sorry he had ever been born? Would she not have forgiven him?

Thinking these thoughts, he let his feet carry him away from his home. His mother had said he was only a burden there. She had said he was not worth the food he ate. All right, he would go away. Perhaps the Masai, who were no longer enemies (though they still stole goats), would like to have him. They were strong people. They lived on cow's blood and milk, because Ngai would not let them till the soil. Everyone knows there is magic in blood and milk; that must be why the Masai were taller and stronger than the Kikuyu people. Once they had been great warriors, before the foreigners had come and stopped their fighting. Mogo could see himself living with them, painting his skin and hair red with clay, as they did. He would wear clothes made of animal skins and carry a spear and a shield. One day he would be as tall as they were, and then he would go home to his mother, and she would see that he was not "as useless as an empty bean pod." She would be sorry then for all those things she had said. So he would go away, far away, to the Rift Valley, where the Masai lived. There she would not be able to find him.

Mogo walked slowly away from his home, along the red road, looking back. But no one shouted "Mogo, Mogo, don't leave us!" Maita did not rush out of the house to cry "Mogo, my lips said what my heart did not feel. . . ."

So he walked on. He passed many huts. People greeted him.

"Peace to you, poor Mogo. Give us a tune!" But he only waved his hand and walked on. There was no music in his heart.

It would be a long walk to the Rift Valley, and he was hungry. He had missed his dinner. Of course he knew anybody in the village would give him something to eat if he asked for it. People would be pointed at if they had no food to spare for a child. But Mogo did not want to be questioned. At last the pain in his empty stomach made him go to a hut and ask for posho. He was given some by a busy mother who was so intent on her many noisy children that she asked no questions at all.

Feeling much better, he followed the red road. Near the edge of the village some children were cutting grass.

"What are you doing?" he asked. They were young children —the older ones were at school.

"We are cutting grass for a new roof for Wacheera because she says the moon shines on her face at night," said a little girl. "Do you want to help us?"

"I have no knife," said Mogo.

"You can have mine, and then I can rest," said the little girl.

Mogo took it. Part of his duty was to help his tribe. Well, these children were of his tribe. But it was hard work. His back got tired from bending, and he did not know very well how to handle the curved knife.

The children were singing a song:

> "Let your knife bite at the grass, ho! ho!
> Snip it off at the roots, ho! ho!
> To cover old Wacheera, ho! ho!
> Or she'll tear out your hair, ho! ho!"

Mogo sat down to rest. He took out his flute and began to play an accompaniment to the song. He thought the children would go on working, but instead they threw down their knives and gathered around him to listen.

"Music, music," they cried. "It's poor Mogo, he can play many tunes!"

Several boys who were herding goats nearby came running to listen too. Soon Mogo had quite an audience.

Ha, he thought. Who is as useless as an empty bean pod *now!* He played for a long time. The children clapped their hands and danced until an angry woman came running up the road, kicking up dust with her flat, bare feet.

"Look at all you idlers," she screeched. "How will my roof be mended this way? Am I never to have any sleep? And what will happen when the rains come? Do you want me to drown, or be washed out of my own house? It's that good-for-nothing Mogo that's keeping you from your work. Go back home, Mogo. Go, we don't want you here."

The children were sorry, but Mogo put his flute in his hair and marched off. All right, so he wasn't wanted there either. All the more reason to go to the Rift Valley. The trouble was that he did not think he would reach it before nightfall. He'd have to find a place to sleep first. Not everybody had room for an extra person. Then he remembered old Wangari, who had wanted him to play for her yesterday. She would have room, for she lived all alone. She might even welcome him.

So he walked on until he came to the old woman's house.

"Old woman of my tribe," he said, "I am on my way to the Masai, but there is no time to reach them before the night. Can I stay with you?"

The old woman hung over her stick. "Will you play for me, then, young bringer-of-dreams? I need sleep, sleep, much sleep, and it will not come. No, no, I cannot find them, my dreams. They have fled and left me. Everyone has left me. Play for me, young man, and you may do what you like."

Mogo played and the old woman listened with nodding head.

After a while her head stopped nodding and began to sink sideways. Her mouth opened and showed her toothless gums. The old woman slept. Mogo hoped she was dreaming.

He stopped playing and looked around. It was not a very nice hut to sleep in. It was dirty. No one seemed to have swept it for ages. It smelled of toadstools. There were holes in the roof where the grass had rotted away. Spiders had woven webs, not only up high in the roof, which was normal, but low down, where Mogo's mother would have chased them away with her stick. Mogo remembered the beauty and order of his own home, and it was as if there was something in his throat he could not swallow.

He went outside to gather some banana leaves to make his bed. But when he went to spread them on the floor of the hut, it was so dusty he took a branch to sweep it first. Then he noticed the fire was going out. He wanted no more bad luck that day and gathered some sticks to put on it. Already it was getting dark.

Mogo looked at the old woman. She was snoring now. Maybe she would sleep forever. He lay down on the banana leaves and shivered. He felt as if he were the only pip left in a big empty gourd.

At home now the oil lamp would be lit. Mother would be serving the evening meal. Karanja and Kimani would have come home, and so would Kunia, with the goats. The goats would have been pushed into their own place in the hut, behind a wall of sticks. They might be bleating a little. The goats would miss him, especially Thaai. At the thought of Thaai, a tear rolled down Mogo's nose. He would never see Thaai again, for goats did not live long. When he returned from the Masai, Thaai would be dead. Another tear followed the first tear.

Perhaps his father would ask for him. "Oh, Mogo," his mother would say. "He is as useless as an empty bean pod. I threw him out." What would Njoki say? Njoki would not like it. She did not think he was useless. . . .

At that moment, just as if he had called up her spirit, Njoki's voice came floating to him from the road.

"Mogo! Mogo! Where are you?"

There was a rustle of banana leaves as Mogo jumped up. The old woman was still sleeping. Mogo ran past her, ran down her corn patch, over the red road, straight to Njoki.

"Here I am," he cried.

"We have all been looking for you," said Njoki. "Why did you run away?"

"Mother said she was sorry I was born. She said I was a burden." Mogo's voice wavered for he felt he was much to be pitied.

"Son of our mother, you are so big a burden that an elephant could not carry you," said Njoki. "Don't you know that our mother has a soft heart and grieves even when such as you are absent?"

"I did not know that." Mogo felt comforted and a little ashamed. Truly, he thought, a boy's mother is like a second god.

"Come, then," said Njoki, giving him her hand. "I, too, want you home."

It did not take them long to walk back, and yet Mogo had felt so very far away.

# THE
# MONKEYS

Mogo was ill for a few days after he ran away. His mother said it all came from his trying to escape his thahu. If he had not tried to help her, she would not have been angry with him and he would not have got ill. Never, never was he to mind the house for her again. She cosseted him, wrapped him in shawls, and made him drink herb teas. He began to think that it was true that he had been foolish. A thahu is a thahu—you can't act as if it were not there.

When he was better he still tried a few times to do what the Mundo-Mugo had advised him. He tried to join the boys of his riika when they were playing games, but they said he was too slow and clumsy, he had better stay with the younger children. The only time he was welcome among them was when he played his flute.

"You see," he told Njoki, "it's just as I said. All I can do is

44

play the flute. No one even *wants* me to be different. It's impossible."

Njoki shrugged her shoulders. "Lazy people want their comfort first and trouble after," she muttered obstinately.

One fine day, Njoki, Mtoto, and Mogo had gone into the woods to shelter from the heat. Mogo had been playing for a while and monkeys had come to listen. They had been so funny in their curiosity and had romped around so foolishly, imitating Mogo and chattering at him, that the children had laughed heartily.

Now they were tired. Njoki and Mtoto were lying on the ground, playing with grasses and flowers. Mogo dozed off. The flute fell out of his hands. He leaned his head against a tree trunk and wandered off into a dream.

He was walking through the Rift Valley, herding his father's goats. All around were the wide spaces where zebras run and giraffe nibble at thorn trees. Suddenly two Masai warriors appeared with painted faces, carrying spears. When they saw Mogo they began to laugh.

"Why do you laugh?" he asked. "What is wrong with me?"

"Ha, ha!" they cried. "You are the boy that cannot carry a spear!"

"You are mistaken," he answered. "I can carry a spear very well." He took the spear they handed him. It was quite light and he held it easily.

"See?" he said. The Masai only laughed more.

"It is not a spear," they cried. "It is only a flute." Mogo looked, and it was true. It was only his flute he was holding.

"Let me try again," he said, but the same thing happened. The Masai mocked him and went away. Then a leopard sprang from behind a rock. It jumped at Thaai. Thaai bleated for help. Mogo waved his flute.

"Go away," he told the leopard.

"Ha, ha," said the leopard. "You can't hurt me with a flute. Now I am going to devour Thaai. . . ."

With a yell Mogo woke up.

"Where am I?" he asked, blinking. Njoki had heard his cry and came to him.

"You were dreaming," she said.

"Yes, I dreamed that my flute . . . where is my flute?" He felt in his hair. He got up and shook his clothes. He looked on the ground. "Where is my flute?" he cried. "Did you take it, Njoki? Njoki, give it to me. You hid it while I slept. Give it to me. Don't tease me, please give it to me. . . ."

But Njoki looked sorrowful.

"I would not tease you," she said. "I haven't got it." Then she glanced up and saw a monkey holding the flute in his mouth.

"There's the thief," she said. "One of the monkeys took it."

"My flute!" cried Mogo. "Give it back, give it back. . . ." But the monkey was crunching the flute between his teeth. He spat out pieces of it. Then he dropped it.

Mogo picked it up. It was ruined. Never, never would it make music again.

"My beautiful, beautiful flute," he sobbed.

"Perhaps it can be repaired," said Njoki. Mogo shook his head. "It's only fit for the hyenas, now," he said. "It's quite dead." They dug a hole and buried it.

"You know, it wasn't a monkey that took it," said Mogo thoughtfully.

"Yes, it was," argued Njoki. "I saw it, and so did you."

"No, it was my ancestor. The Mundo-Mugo warned me. It is my own fault. Oh, what will I do without my flute?" A sob shook him.

"Karanja will make you another one," Njoki promised, pierced by Mogo's grief.

"What is the use?" said Mogo. "My ancestor will only take it away again. I know why, too. I had a dream."

"What was the dream?" asked Njoki.

"It was a dream to show me that there are times when playing the flute won't help me. I must learn other things. Oh, but Njoki, how shall I walk day after day without my flute?"

"They say that when the hyena is robbed of one meal he'll find another," Njoki said consolingly. "Perhaps it will not be so bad after all."

"It will be very bad," muttered Mogo, and after that he did not speak again. They walked home in silence.

At first Mogo grew thin as a cornstalk because he could no longer pour his heart into a flute. His mother feared he would become ill. He could not eat her thick posho, so she coaxed him with mashed avocado pears and slices of juicy pineapple. She consoled him with words too.

"Oh, son of my longing," she said, "do not grieve so much. Your ancestor has a heart. He will not deprive you forever. Your father will give you a little corner in our shamba where you will learn to grow beans and corn. Then you can sell them in the market and buy a better flute there than Karanja could make."

"My ancestor will not permit it," said Mogo with hanging head.

"Yes, he will," his mother told him firmly. "No ancestor would rob a boy of the fruit of his own hands. That much I know. So you work hard and you'll see that I'm right."

That gave Mogo hope again. It also seemed to give him strength. The longing for a flute gave power to his muscles. It was like a whip, driving him on. He was up early, digging his patch of land, for the rains had begun—a few showers at first, and then more and more, soaking the thirsty earth with their silver spears.

Now it was planting time.

"A great honor has befallen us," Mogo's mother told her family at suppertime when they were gathered around the oil lamp. "I have been chosen as Mother of the Village. The seeds will be under my roof the night before the planting."

"That should bring us luck," said Father.

"I was talking to your father, the elder," Mother told him. "He wants to lead the planting ceremony himself, and do it on Mogo's patch of land."

"Does he know about my land?" asked Mogo, opening his eyes wide.

"Yes, I told him. You and Njoki are to take part in the ceremony and carry the sacred digging sticks."

"How kind of my father," said Mogo's father. "He'll stay with us the night, then?"

"Yes, and Njoki, you're to help me clean the house, for the

49

women will be bringing in their seeds. We'll put some of the goats out to make room."

Mogo's grandfather came early the next evening to stay the night. The children were delighted. He was a kind old man; you would not know that he was rich and important from the way he behaved.

"Here is my little bride," he said jokingly to Njoki. "And here is Mogo, the big man who is planting crops for the first time in his life. Ah, that is a great occasion. I was six years old when I planted my first melon seeds. I thought the melons would be round and ready on the ground the next morning. It was a hard lesson for me to have to wait while nature did its work. But never mind, soil does not cheat a man. In the long run we are rewarded."

Early the next morning, Grandfather woke Njoki. "Come, my bride," he said. "Open the door and be the first to leave the house." Every family has its lucky door-opener. In Mogo's family it was Njoki. It is of the greatest importance to have the door opened by the right person in the morning; otherwise an evil spirit might enter.

Now the family went in procession to Mogo's patch of ground. First Grandfather, the elder, then Mogo's parents, carrying the seeds, and Mogo and Njoki with the sacred digging sticks. Karanja and Kimani followed, carrying Mtoto. Many people had gathered to witness the ceremony. They stood huddled in the rain, protecting themselves with shawls and large leaves. No one spoke a word.

Arrived at Mogo's shamba, Grandfather took the seeds, and

looking up at Mount Kere-Nyaga, he raised his hands and said:

> "Holder of Brightness
> Who sent us rain,
> We are going to plant our seeds.
> Bless them for us
> That they may bear much fruit."

Then Grandfather took a handful of seeds and gave them to Mogo's mother, who divided them between Mogo and Njoki.

The children took their digging sticks and broke the ground. Then they planted the seeds. The ceremony was over. The people went home, taking their seeds with them. Grandfather blew the ceremonial horn so that the lazy people who had stayed in bed would know that they could now start planting their shambas. The sacred digging sticks were put by for the next festival.

# THAAI

It seemed to Mogo as if his patch of land were holy now, because it had been blessed by Ngai.

When the first plants began to sprout, Mogo watched them anxiously. He only half believed that they would grow for him the way they grew for Mother and Njoki. But they did. When weeds began to intrude, pushing up greedy green tongues, Mogo pulled them out. He weeded and hoed so industriously that his father's face split in a wide grin as he said to his wife, "There is something in our third son after all."

Mogo began to feel better. The unaccustomed exercise was strengthening his whole body. He began to take joy in movement. At first he joined the play of the younger children, but after a while the boys of his own riika welcomed him. He was never very good and he did not win any games, but he tagged along and the other boys clapped him on the back and said he was doing fine.

53

He learned to shoot arrows and throw spears. His chest widened and his muscles began to curve.

But now and again his longing for music was like the bite of an empty stomach.

Then something happened that took all his attention. Thaai fell ill. Kunia, the herd boy, said he had eaten a poisonous herb, but Mogo's father did not believe it.

"You've counted my goats," he said. "I know well you have, for you are too lazy to remember their names or their faces. You counted them to save yourself trouble and now see what bad luck you've brought on us . . . my best goat!"

It was useless for Kunia to protest that he hadn't, that he would not think of doing such a thing, that he knew it angered the spirits to count possessions . . . Mogo's father did not believe him.

"I shall have to teach you to herd my goats," he told Mogo with a sigh. "You are so much stronger now, I think you could do it. I don't trust Kunia—he has a flighty mother."

Mogo's heart swelled inside him. To hear such words from his father! To be told that his father would trust him rather than tall, lithe Kunia with his flashing teeth! It was happiness such as even his flute had never given him.

But soon he was sad again, because of Thaai. The poor animal was suffering and would not eat. Never had Mogo so longed for his flute; he felt sure he could have quieted Thaai's fever with soothing music. As it was, he did the best he could. Because of the rains it was damp and chilly inside the hut, but Mogo put Thaai on his own bed of dry grass and covered him with his

54

own blankets. Then he sat cross-legged beside him, stroking his wiry coat and calling him the softest names in the Kikuyu language.

Now and again, Njoki arrived with a juicy weed to tempt Thaai to eat, but all he would do was sip a little water, and that only when Mogo held the gourd.

Several days passed. Mogo got little sleep and his parents were anxious.

"Give me a calabash of that new honey beer you made," Mogo's father told his wife heavily. "I shall go to the Mundo-Mugo for a charm to take off the thahu Kunia brought on us."

Mogo's head ached and his eyes felt heavy, but when he heard his father say that, he took courage. The Mundo-Mugo was wise beyond dreaming . . . had he not foretold exactly what was going to happen to Mogo?

He stroked the goat's head and murmured, "It's all right now. You'll soon be better. Father has gone to the Mundo-Mugo."

It was just as if Thaai understood. He seemed a little livelier, and when Njoki came in with a bunch of his favorite herbs, he snuffled at it. Mogo coaxed him to have a nibble.

"He is better," said Njoki. "And it is you who have done it, Mogo, by sitting up with him. You have magic, yourself, Elder Brother!"

"Don't talk like a monkey, Younger Sister," said Mogo. "I have no magic."

Njoki looked stubborn and shut her lips tight.

When Mogo's father returned with a medicine made of herbs the goat was already much improved, and after he had been made to swallow the bitter medicine, he seemed even stronger.

He ate some millet porridge in the evening, and that night Mogo could sleep, stretched out beside Thaai, for the goat was comfortable.

The next day his father drew him aside.

"Third son," he said, "you are growing. I have watched you take care of that goat and I am pleased. The Mundo-Mugo told me, when he gave me the medicine, that it was not really necessary. 'Your son has already cured your goat,' he said. I could see, though he was not so foolish as to praise you, that he did not think ill of you. So I've decided, my son, that it is time you moved into the men's hut."

Mogo felt himself grow warm from his toes to his ears. "T-t-to sleep?" he stammered. "W-with you and K-K-Karanja and K-K-Kimani?"

"Naturally," said his father. "Are you not my son?" After that Mogo held his head a little higher, so that people remarked that they had never seen a boy grow so fast so suddenly.

Mogo had not thought he could be happy while parted from his flute. Truly, Njoki had been right when she said that a hyena robbed of one meal finds another.

Though he felt a little sad at leaving his familiar sleeping place in Mother's hut, it was a great adventure to change to the men's hut.

After supper in Mother's hut, Mogo would now go with his father and brothers to their hut, where visitors often dropped in and gossiped or told stories. His mother had told stories too while she was preparing food or making clay pots, but they were not like the stories Mogo heard now, sitting at his father's fire while the rain whispered outside and the flames flung dark shadows high up against the mud walls where the cobwebs swayed.

Mogo's uncle was there the first evening, the uncle Mogo called "Younger Father."

Younger Father seemed very surprised to see Mogo.

"Is this grasshopper going to sleep here?" he asked. Father did not take him seriously; he only laughed. But Younger Father looked stern and said, "Have you caught a lion yet, Mogo?"

"No," said Mogo. "I have never even *seen* one."

Younger Father cast up his eyes in horror. "When I was young you'd have to have attended at least *one* lion hunt before you were allowed to sleep with the men! I don't know what this generation is coming to."

"There aren't enough lions to go around any more," said Father, coming to Mogo's defense.

"That's true . . . they are dying out. Perhaps that's why boys sit with their noses in books now. They'll soon forget all the skills and knowledge of their tribe."

"They learn new magic," said Father.

"I would *like* to go on a lion hunt," interrupted Mogo. "But no one will take me."

"Too bad," said Younger Father. "You're not a man until you've met your lion."

"Stop it, Kanyita," said Father. "The boy believes every word you say. You'd better tell him one of your good stories."

"Very well," said Younger Father. "I'll tell him how it came about that the mole fears the sun. It happened a long time ago, of course. You can't expect people to believe something that happened yesterday.

"So, a long, long time ago, the sun discovered a medicine that would make people live forever and would bring even the dead to life. But he needed a messenger to take it to the people. He chose the mole, who was then a very fine fellow with a rich coat.

" 'You take this medicine to the people,' said the sun. 'Then they will live forever, and the animals too, and even the dead will come to life.'

" 'Very well,' said the mole. On his way, he met a hyena who asked him where he was going. The hyena had a way of looking down his nose that made the mole feel small. To make himself bigger he told the hyena of the wonderful medicine he was carrying.

"Oi, oi, thought the hyena. If there are no more dead bodies, what shall I eat? But he did not say this aloud. All he said was, 'I have a better medicine. My medicine does away with all men's enemies. And what good is it to live forever if your enemy lives forever too?'

" 'No good at all,' said the mole. The hyena made him feel so envious that at last he exchanged the sun's medicine for the hyena's.

" 'Ha, ha,' cried the hyena, running away. 'You have given me the sun's medicine and I shall hide it where no one can find it, for I do not want to go hungry!'

"The mole felt deeply ashamed of himself. He knew then that what he held in his paws was only a poison. He had played false to the sun and had let himself be tricked. All he could do was to own up. So he went back to the sun and told him what had happened.

"The sun was very angry. 'You have disobeyed me,' he said. 'I am not going to the trouble of making another medicine. Go and search for the place where the hyena has hidden it. I don't want to see you until you have found it.'

"So ever since then the mole has been digging for the hidden medicine and does not dare to show himself to the sun."

Mogo listened to this tale with greedy ears. He had often wondered why moles dig so deeply and was glad to know the reason. But his eyelids were drooping, and his father sent him to his bed, from where he could still see the dark backs of the men against the firelight and hear the murmur of their talk.

I'm going to meet a lion, he thought, as soon as I possibly can. And then I too will be a man. Smiling, he fell asleep.

# THE
# MARKET

The long rains were over, and the sun shone again day after day without winking. Mogo had been learning to herd the goats. His father was pleased to see how unerringly he picked out their goats from the herd. There was no fear of his ever counting them! But there were other things to be learned. Mogo had to know the different calls with which birds warn you that danger threatens. He had to know which plants were good for goats and which were not. He also had to know the footprints of the leopard and the lion.

One day Mogo's new knowledge led him into a dangerous adventure. He and Njoki had been to visit their grandparents, and on the way back Mogo saw the footprints of a lion. Instead of hurrying home as he should have done, he stood and looked at them.

"I've never seen a lion," he said. "Younger Father has told me you have to meet a lion if you want to be a man."

"Then you need weapons," said Njoki.

"But I do not want to kill him," said Mogo. "Younger Father says lions are dying out. I want them to live."

"Then you must not meet them," Njoki pointed out. "It's too dangerous."

"It is the middle of the day," said Mogo. "Lions are sleepy then, and they have eaten. Also, the wind is against us, so they won't smell us. Don't you want to see a lion, Njoki?"

"I do," admitted Njoki.

"We won't go close," promised Mogo.

"This is fun," he whispered as they followed the footprints, trying not to make any noise. "Isn't it fun?"

"Scary fun," said Njoki.

They had meant to stay a good distance away from the lion, but before they knew it, they were almost upon him. Reeds had hidden him from their eyes. Mogo pushed them aside and gasped. There he was, a royal beast with a magnificent mane, drinking peacefully from the river. A little farther on they saw a lioness with three cubs.

They watched for a while, holding their breath. Then they inched back gently, taking care that not a twig crackled.

Later, when they walked on the path again, a little shaky from the danger they had been in, Mogo told Njoki not to talk about their adventure.

"We'd better keep it a secret," he said. "I don't think we'd be admired for it."

Mogo worked hard in his garden. It was clean of weeds, and the bean tendrils drooped with swollen pods. Mogo's eyes glittered when he thought of the beautiful flute he would buy. He

wanted a flute like Mama, his other uncle, had. Mama had
come to visit Mother one day. Mother was his sister. Mogo had
taken the goats to a nearby pasture (he was not yet allowed to go
far), and upon returning home he heard sounds that made him
leap into the air and run. Sounds of a flute! Was it Karanja?
He seldom played now. Instead, Mogo saw his uncle sitting
under the eucalyptus tree, playing gay music while Njoki and
his mother danced. Yes, his mother was dancing!

Mogo stared. Then he hung around his uncle's neck, asking
for more tunes, many, many tunes. His uncle let him try the
flute. It was one bought in a store, made of gleaming dark wood.
It felt like silk between his fingers, and its tones were like
melting honey.

"How well you play!" said his uncle, astonished. "Let me
hear more . . . you have magic."

Mogo played a few tunes, which made his uncle shake his
head in wonder. Then he stopped.

"My ancestor will be angry if I go on playing," he said. Mama
wanted to know why, and Mother told him, for Mogo could not
speak. It had been so hard for him to give up the flute.

Mother also spoke of Mogo's garden and how Mogo hoped to
buy a flute with the money he got from the beans.

"Well, now, that is fortunate," Mama said. "My work is to
drive a truck for a coffee plantation and I'll be going to the
market very soon. I can give Mogo and his beans a lift."

"Oh, *thank* you," said Mogo. Then he saw Njoki's face. They
had planned to go together.

"Will you take Njoki too?" he asked.

Mama had also seen Njoki's face. "All right, then," he agreed. "But it will be a squeeze."

Njoki's smile was like a lit candle. For she was a bit lonesome now that Mogo had gone to his father's hut and played with boys of his own riika. She was glad that no one called him "poor Mogo" any more, but now she felt like "poor Njoki." So she was glad that Mogo had remembered their plan of going to the market together.

Both Njoki's and Mogo's gardens had been fruitful. But when Mogo capered about excitedly, stroking the bags and baskets of beans, bananas, and melons, and singing to himself of the lovely flute they would buy, his father's voice stopped his antics.

"You can't buy a flute with your first earnings," he said.

"Why not?" Mogo stood stiff with fear.

"Because it would not be right. You must buy a goat or a lamb with your first earnings or you'll never be rich."

Mogo wanted to be rich, but there would be nothing left for a flute if he bought a goat or a lamb at the market, and he could not bear to wait for another harvest before he had his flute. Tears stood in his eyes, and he looked so forlorn that his father smiled.

"I did not mean to alarm you," he said. "I just wanted to tell you that I'll sell you Thaai for one of your big melons."

Mogo threw himself at his father and hugged him.

"Oh Baba, Baba, *thank* you. . . ." To have Thaai for his very own and still be able to buy a flute with his beans! He felt like a pot that is boiling too fast and bubbling over.

On the day Mama came to fetch the children they were waiting for him, their harvests neatly packed. Mogo had clean shorts on, and Mother had washed Njoki's dress and combed her hair with a long-toothed comb. They had both brushed their teeth with a stick of frayed wood. But Njoki's neck was bare. Whenever Mogo saw it he felt guilty. She had given him her necklace and he ought to buy her another. Perhaps the next harvest. . . .

Mother waved them off as they went. "Bring back a luckpenny!" she cried.

The ride in the truck was delightful. The children sat high up, beside their uncle. The truck went fast, sometimes purring like a big cat and then again snarling and growling like a wild dog. Mogo watched his uncle do mysterious things with handles and a big wheel.

"What makes the truck go without an animal to pull it?" he asked. "Is it magic?"

"It's a kind of magic," Mama admitted. "But it's not the magic of spirits, it's the magic of things."

"Could I learn it?" asked Mogo.

"You could learn to use it, like me," said Mama. "But if you want to understand it you have to go to school. It's the foreigners who know about this magic."

"Perhaps I'll be strong enough to go to school next year. Look at my arm," said Mogo, who was proud of his swelling muscles.

"What is Njoki going to buy with what she gets for her beans?" asked Mama, who had noticed that Njoki was very quiet.

"I am going to buy a necklace," said Njoki. "The girls of my riika all have lovely beads to put on . . . and they ask me why I have none."

64

"You did not tell me that," said Mogo.

"I did not want to tell you because I am glad I gave you my necklace. But now I have so many beans I am going to buy one. Then I'll look the same as the other girls."

Some of the joy left Mogo's heart. He had thought only of his flute. He had not known that Njoki missed her beads. It was not right that he had not thought of that.

As they came nearer the market they saw many women with large burdens on their heads and backs. Sometimes a woman had a great basket on her head, and on top of it, a little baby. There were also men leading cows or loaded donkeys.

The truck roared past them all, leaving them to toil on slowly, like snails.

Mogo and Njoki had been to the market before. Their uncle put them down at a place where they could spread their wares. He had to leave them there but promised he would fetch them when their shadows were smallest. At present their shadows still stretched long before them.

The children loved the market. There was such noise and bustle there! Many different kinds of people walked around, all looking for bargains, and vendors shouted praises of their wares. There was such an overflowing of wealth and color, such gaiety of dress and drapery, and over it all hung the fine foliage of trees, sifting the rays of the sun into dancing patterns.

Mogo found a buyer for his beans and received a handful of shillings. Njoki was still bargaining in halting Swahili with a lady who did not want to pay her price. Finally she too received her money.

Now they were free to wander around. Njoki wanted to

see necklaces, and Mogo was impatient to find a flute. They quarreled a little about which to do first and finally decided to separate.

"We'll meet again there," said Njoki, pointing at a place where a lot of big pots were for sale. It was easy to see from a distance.

Mogo hurried off, repeating to himself the Swahili word for *flute* that his uncle had taught him. The difficulty about the market was that people spoke many different languages. Swahili was the bridge between one language and another, but few people knew it well.

Mogo looked for musical instruments. There were drums for sale with lovely patterns on them. There were bells to tie round your ankles when dancing, as well as cymbals and horns. At last he found some flutes, but they were heavy and expensive. There was one like his uncle's, only not so good, and it cost many shillings. Mogo thought he would look around some more. He still hadn't found what he wanted when he passed the place where the pots were on sale. There he saw Njoki, looking for him, her cheeks dripping with tears. He ran to her, ducking between people.

"What is the matter, Njoki?" he asked.

"I . . . I do not understand . . ." sobbed Njoki. "I . . . I saw a necklace on a s-s-stand, and there . . . there was a lady standing beside it. I . . . I asked . . . asked her for the necklace and she said 'give me your money, then I'll wrap it up for you.' I g-gave her the money and she disappeared. There is a man who says he is the one who sells the n-necklace and he g-g-got no money

66

so he won't give it to me. He says the l-lady was a thief . . . and
. . . and now I have no money for all my beans!''

"We may still find her," said Mogo, clenching his fists. "What
did she look like?"

"I d-d-don't remember . . . I was looking at the b-beads.
They were so p-pretty. I don't like it here," she went on fiercely.
"Take me home, Mogo. This is a wicked place where people
tell untruths and take money they have not worked for. I never
want to go to the market again!"

"Our shadows are not small enough yet," said Mogo. "We
must wait for Mama." He was clenching his shillings so tightly
they cut the palm of his hand. There was a strong pain in his
heart. He knew there was something he must do, but he felt

he could not do it. Then he looked at Njoki, whose eyelashes were sticky with tears and who still shook now and then with sobs. He would have no shillings at all if it had not been for her. He would still be sleeping in his mother's hut like a ninny, unable to herd the goats or raise beans.

"Never mind, Njoki," he said, putting his arm round her. "Perhaps that woman had hungry children. Perhaps she needed those shillings more than we do. I did not see a flute I wanted, so instead I'll buy you a necklace."

Njoki wiped away her tears. Her teeth and eyes shone in a smile.

"Oh, will you?" Then she faltered. "But I forgot . . . your flute. You must have your flute."

"No," said Mogo firmly, grasping his pain as if it were a nettle. "Probably my ancestors would not even want me to have it. I owe you a necklace, Njoki, I do . . . and I'm sorry I did not know that it made you look different from the other girls not to have one . . . and that they noticed it. I didn't think you missed it."

Mogo knew well the misery of not being like the others.

The pain in his heart seemed to have gone. There was only pride left that he could dry Njoki's tears and put dimples in her cheeks with the fruits of his own labor.

"Do you want to show me that necklace you chose?" he asked.

Njoki shook her head. "I do not like it any more," she said. "It makes me think of the thief."

"Then we must go and look for another one together," Mogo said gravely. "I'll take care you're not cheated again. We'll go to the very best stall."

68

They looked around for a long time until they saw a pretty lady who was selling the most beautiful beads. She was a Kikuyu lady, so they could consult with her and exchange many words to get her opinion as to which was the best, most flattering necklace.

"Though it is Ngai who gives beauty, we must help him, mustn't we?" she said.

"It doesn't matter about the price," Mogo told her grandly. "I've plenty of money."

Njoki finally chose beads that shone in many different colors, like soap bubbles. You could look at them for a long time without tiring of them. There was some money left, so Mogo bought a bracelet for his mother as well.

When Mama came with his truck, two cheerful children greeted him. This surprised him, for when they told him what had happened it seemed to him that they had met with very bad luck. He shook his head over it. "It teaches you," he told Njoki, "never to trust anyone until you've finished a bag of salt with him."

But Mogo knew now what the Mundo-Mugo had meant when he had said that a bad thing could be a good thing too. He still had a pain in his heart, but it was the happiest pain he had ever had in his life.

# THUNDERSTORM

Mogo's ancestors must have been pleased with him at last. For, several weeks after that market day, Mama came on a visit and brought a present for Mogo. It was wrapped in a banana leaf. When Mogo unrolled it, he found Mama's flute.

Mogo wanted to say many things. He wanted to say how pleased he was and how grateful . . . but he could only look, and clasp the flute. No sound came out of his mouth.

Mama patted his head.

"You have a great gift," he said. "You need a flute. I am getting too old to play it. Flutes are for young people."

Since Mogo could not speak, his mother said all the things he should have said. And then she added, "He deserves it. He has been so good. Look at the beautiful bracelet he bought me with his own earnings!"

It seemed to Mogo that he was dreaming it all. He wandered

off with his flute, expecting to wake up when he tried to play it, as had happened in his other dreams. But when he started to play, the music came rolling out of his flute, deep and true like the sound of his grandfather's horn. He knew then that he was awake and that his flute was as real as the jacaranda tree which was scattering its blue blossoms at his feet.

So he played and played that evening, drinking in the music as the earth drinks the water of the first rains. All the things he had not been able to say poured out of his flute; he blew away all his longings, he freed the feelings that had been locked up for long months in his heart, transformed them into fountains of song that seemed to reach to the skies.

No one came near him. His family knew that he had to be alone with his flute.

But afterwards Mogo was able to put his flute aside. He had Thaai to look after as well as his father's goats. He had friends now, too, who came to fetch him for a game or a tussle. He had his shamba, a bigger one this time. He could not neglect all these things to play the flute. They had become valuable to him also.

So he only played in his free time. Even so, his playing was improved. Partly because of the better flute, of course. But also because Mogo had grown, and it showed in his music.

Thaai, of all the goats, loved music best, so Mogo invented a special song for him. It was a song in which he praised Thaai as the cleverest and strongest animal on earth. Since his song had no words, the spirits could not get angry at it.

Now came the great day when Father was to dismiss Kunia

71

as his herdsboy and give the job to Mogo. For the first time Mogo would be away for the whole day, with the other herds-boys. His mother packed a lunch of posho for him in a banana leaf.

"Remember to come back safe and well," she told him jok-ingly, "or I'll change you into a bird."

Kunia had found another villager to employ him, so he was with the herdsboys. He was not friendly to Mogo because he was angry that Mogo's father had dismissed him. Mogo's father had paid him better than his new master did. Kunia made the other boys less friendly too. Mogo felt that they were all treat-ing him as if he did not belong to their riika. He was not as tall as they were, of course, but he was tough now and could take care of himself. But under Kunia's leadership the boys kept asking him if he wasn't getting tired, and explaining things he knew very well. It was useless to get angry. Mogo had to be with them all day.

But he enjoyed herding despite the boys. He liked roaming from one forest clearing to another, behind the frisky goats with their perky tails and curved horns. Mogo held his herding stick firmly and did what his father had told him to do. He watched out for poisonous plants or the footprints of leopards, and he also kept a wary eye open for thieving Masai or Kipsigis, who sometimes descended upon a herd, brandishing spears, and carried off the best beasts.

When it was time for their meal, the boys all lay on the grass and ate their cold posho, picking it out of banana leaves with their fingers. Mogo played a tune on the flute for them, and that made the other boys friendly, but not Kunia. Kunia told Mogo not to play, it could bring bad luck. The other boys all cried that that was nonsense, that it was only inside a hut you must not play, but Kunia was sure he'd heard herdsmen tell of evil spirits being attracted by a flute and damaging the herd. It frightened the other boys, so Mogo stuck the flute in his hair and did not take it out again.

Then the boys played games for a while. They divided into two groups. Kunia was the leader of one group, Mogo was the last-chosen in the opposite group. One game was to see who could make the fattest boast.

"The earth belongs to us," shouted Kunia's group.

"And the sky belongs to us," answered Mogo's group.

"We own the sun."

"And we the rain . . ."

"We own the mountains . . ."

"We the earthquakes . . ."

The game ended in a fight; they all rolled in the grass and felt much better.

But the goats had meanwhile wandered off. They were heading for the sacred tree, where the elders made sacrifices to Ngai. This was such a holy place that no ordinary person would come near it, except when there was a ceremony and the elders were there. But, of course, goats have no sense. The boys called to them and ran to head them off. The goats got confused and scampered in many directions. It took a long time for the boys to get them all together again, and they were warm from running. As they sat down to rest, panting and wiping their foreheads with dry grass, Mogo heard the three clear notes of the rainbird. He looked up at the sky. Clouds were massing at the horizon.

"I think we should be going home," he said.

"It's too early," Kunia objected in a superior tone. "The goats won't get fat that way."

"I think it is going to rain." Mogo pointed to the sky.

"Who is afraid of a shower?" jeered Kunia. "If you are too delicate to stand a wetting, why does your father let you herd goats? We can do without you, can't we, boys?" The other boys looked at their feet. They did not want to take sides.

Mogo shrugged his shoulders. "I'm not afraid," he said. "But it looks like more than a shower to me."

"That's because you are inexperienced," Kunia pointed out. "You're not used to herding, that's all. You'd better take our advice."

Mogo said nothing. He went with the boys to drive the goats into the Rift Valley, where they found many interesting herbs to eat. He still thought Kunia was wrong. The rainbird kept calling insistently, and the clouds were pushing up angry heads. It looked like thunder to Mogo. It is bad to be out in a thunderstorm, for that is when Ngai moves from one mountain to another. That is when he cracks his finger joints to warn his enemies and flashes his bright sword. Woe to the man who sees him—he is struck dead at once. Mogo remembered the commands of his mother every time it thundered: "Come indoors, stay in the hut, don't look at the sky . . . hide your face . . ."

74

A pretty fix they'd be in if thunder overcame them in the Rift Valley . . . where would they hide then?

Without saying anything he began to steer the goats towards the woods that ran down into the Rift Valley at one point. The other boys followed without thinking. The clouds were advancing rapidly. They were slate colored, with frothing tops. And, as if to meet in battle, other clouds drifted toward them from the opposite part of the sky. That only happened when Ngai made ready to move.

Some of the boys were beginning to get alarmed. The sun still shone, but uneasily. Gusts of wind rustled the dry grass. Birds circled overhead with warning cries. Then the sun went, overwhelmed by the clouds. There was a greenish gloom over everything. The valley lay flat and open, like the palm of a hand, to receive the wrath of God.

The boys saw now what Mogo had seen much earlier. They reproached Kunia for not taking Mogo's advice. Kunia had also realized that he had been wrong, but he did not want to admit it.

"Just a shower," he said. "That's all it is." But his voice squeaked.

They were nearing the woods. The clouds were locked in combat. Sparks flashed through the sky. Spears of rain shot down. Everywhere animals were running for shelter. Ngai was growling behind the clouds and beginning to crack his knuckles. The goats stampeded, and the boys ran after them, making for the woods. Ngai's anger raged around them. His sword glittered again and again, lighting up the darkened world. The sky boiled

75

and seethed with clouds, and rain hissed down. The boys could hear the dull thud of hoofs as zebras, giraffe, and perhaps even elephants fled from the storm.

Mogo had shut his eyes and was running blind. He did not want to risk seeing Ngai. He ran against a tree trunk, which knocked out his breath and half stunned him. Then he fought his way deeper into the foliage, panting with fear.

The other boys did much the same thing. Soon they all lay huddled together under the trees, covering their eyes with their hands, making sure that not a gleam of Ngai's brightness could penetrate.

Ngai was making a long journey, much longer than any of the boys had ever lived through. It seemed as if the whistling rain, the loud claps of Ngai's fingers, and the searing of his molten sword would go on forever, but gradually the rumbles grew softer, more distant. The rain no longer lashed the trees but rustled them gently. The sword still flickered faintly in the distance. . . . Then, like a long sigh after weeping, came silence, broken only by the drip-drip-dripping of soaked trees.

One after another the boys raised their heads. They got up, shaking their stiff, wet bodies. Some of the boys took off their shorts and shirts and wrung them out before putting them on again. Mogo made sure that his flute hadn't got wet. He had sheltered it as well as he could. The boys' teeth were chattering with cold, their eyes bloodshot from being pressed against their hands.

"Where are the goats?" asked Mogo. There was not a single one to be seen. The boys began to call their names, but there was no answering bleat or patter of feet. The boys searched, and wherever they went showers of water wetted them anew from the dripping branches.

"They've stampeded, and goodness knows where they've gone," said Kunia. "We could be looking forever this way. We need help. Let's go home. The men can find them much quicker than we can."

"Yes, yes, let's go home," cried the other boys. "It must be late, our mothers will be anxious, and we're frozen."

"And leave the herd?" asked Mogo in a voice as cold as rain.

"Well, we've looked for the creatures and can't find them," said Kunia. "What more can we do? There's no knowing where they've gone. That thundershower lasted for ages."

"It only *seemed* ages," said Mogo. "I don't think it was so long. Anyway, my father's wealth is in those goats. I'm not leaving till I find them."

"That's true. . . ." The other boys began to see it Mogo's way, but Kunia laughed them out of it.

"What does *he* know? It's his first day of herding. He doesn't know a hillock from a buffalo's hump. If he stays behind he is sure to catch cold—or a leopard may kill him, or he may get lost. But perhaps his father cares more for his goats than for his son."

"What's the use of a son who abandons goats that are in his care?" asked Mogo. "Perhaps you have no brave ancestors to worry about, but mine fought lions with their bare hands to defend the herd."

"Ha! Mine were just as brave, but they had sense. They did not give the hyenas two meals when one was enough."

It would not have been much longer before Mogo and Kunia were locked in a fist-fight, and Mogo would have lost, for Kunia was much stronger. But the other boys got impatient.

"Come, then, Kunia, if you are going home," they cried. "We're cold."

"Very well, then, stay if you like," Kunia told Mogo and went off with the others. Mogo listened to their voices and footsteps getting fainter and fainter in the distance. Then he was alone at the edge of a deep, wild forest. He wondered if he had been stupid and stubborn.

He remembered his flute. The boys had thought it would bring bad luck, but Mogo did not believe it. They had had bad luck already, anyway. The boys were gone now. Perhaps his flute would coax the goats out of their hiding places. Thaai would come if Mogo played him his own song.

So Mogo put the flute to his mouth, and its tones pierced the stillness after the storm. As if called by it, the sun burst forth, sending its rays to chase the darkness and warm the shivering valley. The raindrops that still clung to twigs and leaves and blades of grass caught the sunbeams and sent them back in splinters of light that dazzled the eyes. The woods seemed to be hung with brilliant jewels. And Mogo's music matched what his eyes saw. Never had his flute called so richly.

It took time, but Mogo was not impatient. Steadily he spun charms, and the high, sweet tones he flung into the forest probed into its nooks and hidden hollows.

As the flute wheedled and sang, all Mogo's love for Thaai seemed to melt into the music.

"Come Thaai, my first one, my dearest," it said. "Don't

hide any more. Ngai has found his new mountain and is no longer angry. There is nothing to fear and I am here, your Mogo, who loves you and will bring you home. Don't you want to come, Thaai? Do you not smell the grass roof of our hut? There will be posho hot out of the pot, with beans and bananas. I shall share it with you if you will only come, my sweet. I shall rub your wet coat with soft towels and I shall sing you to sleep, Thaai, my love. Come, then, come."

On and on went the flute, until the sun sank down to the horizon with a last farewell kiss to the sky. Then, just when Mogo had lost heart, there was a crashing of foliage and branches, and Thaai came thundering along like a tornado, bringing behind him all the other goats except one, which belonged to Kunia's new master. Later, that one was seen among the herds of the Masai.

Thaai ran straight into Mogo's arms, and Mogo's arms went around the pungent, tickly, wet body.

"Thaai, Thaai," he cried. "You came, you brought them all back, you clever, wonderful Thaai!"

The other goats were looking for their masters and the sooner Mogo got them home the better. So, putting his flute to his lips again (his herd stick was lying forgotten in the woods), he piped a triumphant tune while he and Thaai headed the procession that marched home.

# THE
# FESTIVAL

When the boys came home after the thunderstorm and reported the goats missing, there was great consternation in the village. The boys, fearing to be blamed for leaving the goats to their fate, were so mysterious about their disappearance, the villagers jumped to the conclusion that during the terrible thunderstorm, a more frightening one than any of them could remember, Ngai had taken the goats and swept them up with him on his journey from mountain to mountain, to punish the village for some oversight. The elders of the village went to consult the Mundo-Mugo. A sacrifice might be necessary to propitiate Ngai and get the goats back.

The goats were a great loss to Mogo's family, for Kimani had found a girl he would like to marry, and her parents asked a bride price of many goats. If there were none, Kimani would not be able to marry.

*The Festival*

But with Mogo gone, the family found it hard even to think about the goats. From the boys' strange behavior and Kunia's mysterious words, Mogo's parents thought that he too had been swept up into the clouds. Only Njoki was staunch in disbelieving it.

"Ngai is good. He would not do such a thing," she said, quite boldly, for she had been told since she was a baby not to contradict her parents. But her parents did not punish her, for they were glad to hear a word of comfort.

"It is just those boys. They are lying. They are like the hyenas, with a big noise in front and their tails between their legs at the back. I bet they just left the goats because they were wet and cold. Mogo would not do that. Mogo would stay."

So she was the only one who was not surprised when Mogo came marching into the village, followed by a procession of prancing goats.

The village people heard the flute first: it was like music from heaven, like a bright spirit sent down from the skies to tell them that they were mistaken, Ngai had not punished them. Gay and mischievous and triumphant came the pearly tones, and in between, the ding-dong of the goat bells. The villagers streamed to meet the procession, and great was their relief and joy after so horrid a fear.

Mogo was welcomed into many arms, but his mother's won. She embraced him and rubbed him down with towels and gave him hot herb tea to drink. The rest of his family hovered around him as if he were a lost lamb that had been found. He could not understand it. He had expected to be scolded for not

83

having seen the thunder coming and for not having brought the goats back in time.

"K-Kunia wouldn't believe me," he said, his teeth chattering because of his mother's rubbing. "I t-told him we should go home."

"Kunia is a rascal," grumbled his father.

"Yes, the other b-boys wanted to stay with me, but K-Kunia made them go home," said Mogo.

Meanwhile the villagers were feasting to celebrate the return of their wealth. They lit a fire in an open place and brought corn to roast and other good food to cook. When Mogo was ready to join them, they wanted him to tell them what had happened. Mogo was pulled into the midst of them and had to answer their questions. When the villagers understood how they had been fooled by the other boys, especially by Kunia, they looked around for them, but the boys had disappeared. They had the wits to know they would not be loved at that moment. They were hoping that all would be forgotten presently and they could then creep back and finish the remains of the feast.

So the villagers could not revenge themselves on the boys. Instead they began to praise Mogo.

"That is a boy to be admired," they told his mother. "We did not think much of him at first, always playing the flute, and so thin and puny, but he has shaped up well. It is a great surprise."

"Yes, that Mogo, he stuck it out. The thunder did not chase him away. Someone for his ancestors to be proud of."

"And that flute playing of his, that is not so useless as we thought. It brought our goats back. Yes, yes, the flute is not an idle instrument after all."

Mogo became worried when he heard all these remarks. "Listen to what they are doing!" he said to Njoki. "They are *praising* me! I've just got over the folly of their praising me at birth, and now they are starting it again!"

"Never mind, I'll put a stop to it," said Njoki. She began to shout: "I have a worthless brother! He is no good at all! It is not worth bothering about him!" The other villagers looked surprised at first, but then they caught on.

"Yes, he is a miserable fellow," they said, grinning cheerfully. "What a burden to his parents! We cannot understand why he was allowed to live!" Everyone was laughing, for they knew all the time that they were only fooling the spirits. Mogo felt safe again.

Then there was a commotion. The elders had come back with the Mundo-Mugo. The Mundo-Mugo had already told them that Ngai was not angry. He had gone with them to reassure the village and found the people all celebrating the return of Mogo and the goats. Everyone made way for the Mundo-Mugo. He went straight to Mogo's parents and began to talk to them.

Njoki was there, and afterward she went and told Mogo what she had heard.

"The Mundo-Mugo said that you have music inside you and that when you are older people will come from the four corners of the world to listen to you. He said now that you are stronger, you should go to school. He also said that you must have a music teacher. There are music teachers in the city. Father promised

him that he would sell many goats if necessary. He said if it is
the will of our ancestors that you learn those things, you shall
learn them. I told you that you would be 'wonderful Mogo' one
day! But you will go far away from me, and I shall miss you."

"Ah," said Mogo. "We do not know. Any fool can tell how
many apples there are on a tree, but no one knows how many
trees there are in an apple. Wait and see. Perhaps I shall take
you with me."

"Oh, Mogo, that would be lovely," sighed Njoki. "I could
cook your posho and mend the roof of your house and sweep
your floor . . ."

"That's a long way off," said Mogo, and he took Njoki's
hand and squeezed it.

The Mundo-Mugo was passing from one person to another,
making talk. Mogo was not afraid of him any more.

He went up to him.

"I know the answer to the riddle 'What is good to have,
better to lose, and best to find again?' " he said. "It's my flute."

"Clever boy," said the Mundo-Mugo, nodding. "Yes, for *you*
it was the flute. It's a different thing for each person." He
looked thoughtfully at Mogo. "Your ancestors are pleased with
you." Then he smiled. The Mundo-Mugo did not often smile.
It reminded Mogo of the moment the sun had come out after
the storm.

The Mundo-Mugo went back to his hut in the woods. The
moon came out full and round, and the villagers danced. The
old ones and the young ones, the children and the babies, all
danced in the moonlight to celebrate the return of the goats.

The oil lamps threw patches of orange light through the windows of the huts. The drums beat the usual accompaniment to the dance, but above their deep throbbing soared the golden, jubilant tones of Mogo's flute.